Samuel French Acting Edition

I0591786

A Good Old Fashioned Redneck Country Wedding

by Kris Bauske

SAMUELFRENCH.COM   SAMUELFRENCH.CO.UK

FOR PRODUCTION ENQUIRIES

UNITED STATES AND CANADA
Info@SamuelFrench.com
1-866-598-8449

UNITED KINGDOM AND EUROPE
Plays@SamuelFrench.co.uk
020-7255-4302

Each title is subject to availability from Samuel French, depending
upon country of performance. Please be aware that *A GOOD OLD
FASHIONED REDNECK COUNTRY WEDDING* may not be licensed by
Samuel French in your territory. Professional and amateur producers
should contact the nearest Samuel French office or licensing partner to
verify availability.

MUSIC USE NOTE

Licensees are solely responsible for obtaining formal written permission from copyright owners to use copyrighted music in the performance of this play and are strongly cautioned to do so. If no such permission is obtained by the licensee, then the licensee must use only original music that the licensee owns and controls. Licensees are solely responsible and liable for all music clearances and shall indemnify the copyright owners of the play(s) and their licensing agent, Samuel French, against any costs, expenses, losses and liabilities arising from the use of music by licensees. Please contact the appropriate music licensing authority in your territory for the rights to any incidental music.

IMPORTANT BILLING AND CREDIT REQUIREMENTS

If you have obtained performance rights to this title, please refer to your licensing agreement for important billing and credit requirements.

A GOOD OLD FASHIONED REDNECK COUNTRY WEDDING was first produced by Osceola Arts at the Black Box Theatre in Kissimmee, Florida in July 2013. The cast was as follows:

LOU (LOUISE) WEXLER .... Mary Beth Finley

BILL WEXLER .... Russell Trahan

DAVE FOX .... Chris Kurzer

BARBIE JO FOX .... Erika Remley

JIMMY WEAVER .... Eduardo Rivera

DARLENE FULMER .... Kyra Bauske

SHERIFF LESTER THOMPSON .... James Ball

SHARKY SPINOZA .... Ken Anders

PAULY PIRELLI .... Scott Sheplee

CHARACTERS

LOU (LOUISE) WEXLER – Lou is a bubbling bundle of energy. She takes command of the stage like she takes command of her diner. Mid-thirties, she is attractive, intelligent, and well-respected. Both men and women find value in Lou's many philosophies of life. She has a feminine build and is considered curvy. Her hair and make-up are flawless, and she exudes an air of utter capability. Lou is always moving and dispensing tough, no-nonsense wisdom as she bounces from one task to another throughout the diner she's owned and loved since she was in her early twenties. Lou is energetic hospitality personified. Welcoming – never hillbilly harsh.

BILL WEXLER – Bill is a retired Marine who served in the Middle East and is married to Lou. Mid-to-late thirties, he is taller than the other men, wears his hair in a typical military style, and has an air of authority that is impossible to miss. He owns a trail guiding business, and his physique indicates his athleticism. He grew up in the town of Christmas and loves hiking, fishing, and hunting. If any of the men understand women and relationships, Bill's the man. Bill doesn't take orders from the boys, but his philosophy concerning women is generally to do as Lou says.

DAVE FOX – Dave is a typical married father of two in his thirties who works as a butcher. He is painfully average in looks and intelligence. Dave cultivated his great sense of humor to compensate for his overly average averageness. He loves to crack jokes to avoid any deep discussions. He loves his wife and children, but sometimes he needs a break. Dave and Bill have been friends all their lives, and Jimmy is the butt of many of Dave's jokes because Dave secretly envies Jimmy's free and easy bachelor life.

BARBIE JO FOX – Barbie Jo is the beleaguered wife of Dave and the daughter of Verna Belle. She has two children and Dave to raise. She is attractive but frazzled. She never quite manages to look completely put together. Barbie Jo's mother never lets her forget that she could have married better, gotten a better education, and just generally done better in life if she hadn't married Dave the butcher right out of high school. Barbie Jo works full-time at the diner, and Lou considers Barbie Jo her "right hand girl."

JIMMY WEAVER – Jimmy considers himself the "ladies' man" in town. In his mid-twenties, he is cute and charming, but he isn't terribly smart. He is woefully lacking in any understanding of what women really want from a man. Jimmy's family has owned a hog farm near town for generations, and Jimmy is a real, down-home farm boy. He loves to hunt and fish and basically do whatever he darn well pleases. He is engaged to the town hottie, Darlene. He met Bill and Lou when he started dating Darlene, and Bill and Dave added him to their group right away because he shares their love of women, beer, and most of all, hunting!

DARLENE FULMER – Darlene is an All-American beauty! In her early twenties, she is blonde and built. Darlene wears short skirts and tight sweaters. She is a typical rodeo queen with horses on her mind and cowboys on her tail. No hairstyle is too big, no jewelry too outrageous for Darlene. She is a complete innocent who accepts everything at face value. No one considers Darlene a brain, but what she lacks in smarts, she makes up for in heart. She met Jimmy through an Internet dating service two years ago. Darlene is engaged to Jimmy and is a good-hearted gal who just wants to make the world a better place!

SHERIFF LESTER THOMPSON – Lester is not only the County Sheriff, he is Darlene's cousin and an ordained minister. He is in his forties to fifties and smart. He may sound like a country boy, but Sheriff Lester's got it all going on.

SHARKY SPINOZA – Real gangster-type out of New Jersey. Thirty to fifty and has a strong Jersey accent. This character is cute if he's played by a really short actor and his sidekick, Pauly Pirelli, is played by a big, tall actor.

PAULY PIRELLI – Dumb, harmless gangster-enforcer-type and employee of Sharky. He is Sharky's "muscle" and right-hand man, but he isn't terribly smart. He is instantly smitten with the lovely Darlene. Best if played by a thirty-something, tall, strong actor. The bigger, the better!

SETTING

There is one basic set divided into two sections:

The Diner – Lou's Diner is a typical small-town diner. There are booths and tables on the checkerboard floor. Chrome tables and chairs hailing from the fifties era give the diner an air of authentic nostalgia. The booths run along the front window of the diner. The front door is at the far end near the kitchen. A counter sits at the back of the diner set, and a door and window behind the counter are open into the kitchen area. There is a coat rack in the corner near the front door. A large, cheery cowbell hangs from the door and rings when the door is opened or closed. There are menus in a stack on the counter next to a pile of silverware wrapped in napkins. Napkin dispensers, plastic holders for small containers of cream and jelly, and salt and pepper shakers sit on each table. Every detail is authentic. Vigorously decorated for Valentine's Day.

The Cabin: The hunting cabin is rough and woodsy, not quite chic enough to be called rustic. There is an exterior door at the back of the cabin and a window off to one side. There are no curtains on the window. A bar with two bar stools sits in front of the window. There is a sofa in the center of the room with an old chair off to one side. The arm of the chair appears to have been broken at some point and repaired with duct tape. A hand-crocheted afghan is tossed carelessly over the back of the sofa. An ottoman rests in front of the chair, and a coffee table sits before the sofa. None of these items match, as if placed there more for comfort and usefulness than for appearance. A worn room rug is on the floor under the coffee table. A large moose head hangs on the wall above the door. The cabin is wood-paneled and sparse.

AUTHOR'S NOTES

This play is written in two acts, but it may be produced as a one-act play if it better suits the needs of your theater and audience.

To facilitate the smooth transition from one scene to the next, it is necessary to cross-fade lights between scenes. Never go to black.

ACT I

Scene One

(At rise: Inside Lou's Diner. This is any small-town diner in the mountains. Not fancy, but not shabby either. LOU is an energetic, no-nonsense woman who runs a clean place and dispenses wisdom and advice along with the best food in town. The front door is upstage right. To the rear is a counter with stools. Behind the counter is a serving window that reveals the kitchen.)

(Hanging on the walls are Valentine's Day decorations – red hearts with white lace and lots of pink crepe paper. On the counter are the remnants of a wedding cake. The pieces and parts are scattered about, and one large white section sits otherwise untouched, waiting to be put back together. A pile of unfolded napkins sits on the counter.)

(LOU comes out of the kitchen wearing a fancy bridesmaid's dress covered by a large apron. She is wiping her hands on a towel, and she is not happy.)

LOU. How could you let that dog get Darlene's cake the night before her wedding?

(DARLENE pops up from behind the counter wearing her wedding dress. She has been stacking napkins under the counter. This can be any wedding dress, but it will be truly Darelene-esque if she wears a white mini skirt with a long train in the ridiculous mullet style.)

DARLENE. I don't mind, Lou. I love old Rufus!

(Straightens a crooked heart decoration hanging on the wall.)

Isn't Valentine's Day absolutely the best day for a big, romantic wedding? I can't believe we pulled it together so quickly.

LOU. Big, romantic wedding, and here we sit! We're supposed to be at the church decorating pews and fixing hair! Instead we're here baking cakes!

DARLENE. Mary Sue and Mark are handling the decorations at the church. We'll be fine. What's wrong with my hair? I thought it looked good today. Need more fluffing?

LOU. It's fine. You're perfect.

DARLENE. Barbie Jo, does my hair look like it needs fixin' to you? I got some hairspray in the car.

> *(BARBIE JO working in the kitchen. She can be seen through the kitchen window with her hair pulled up and wearing a bridesmaid's dress identical to LOU's. She is also covered by an oversized apron and continues to mix up a new cake as she speaks.)*

BARBIE JO. Lou's right, Darlene. You're fine. Fixin' hair's just somethin' girls do before the wedding to pass the time.

DARLENE. Instead of baking new cakes, huh?

(Giggles.)

BARBIE JO. I told Dave to chain that dog, but no, he says. He likes to sleep in the house, he says. He needs me, he says.

LOU. The only thing that dog needs is a stomach pump!

(Pause.)

How much'd you say he ate?

BARBIE JO. The top two tiers and part of the groom.

LOU. Good riddance there.

DARLENE. Now, Lou, be nice. Jimmy is my other half – the love of my life.

LOU. Just teasin', Darlene. Jimmy really has settled down. I never thought it would happen.

DARLENE. Of course he has! You heard him at Christmas! Why he couldn't wait for us to be joined as man and wife!

LOU. I remember.

BARBIE JO. Darlene, has Jimmy ever even been in a church?

DARLENE. I'm not sure. Why?

BARBIE JO. Just checking. If he hasn't read the contract, he may be surprised by the requirements of this particular agreement. That's all.

DARLENE. Anyway, I hope old Rufus'll be okay, Barbie Jo. Good thing he didn't eat that bottom piece.

LOU. Why? One more piece wouldn't make much difference!

DARLENE. But it could! That bottom tier is chocolate. Chocolate ain't good for dogs.

BARBIE JO. But two slabs of sponge cake covered in butter cream is?!

DARLENE. I don't know. I never heard nothin' about butter cream. Just chocolate. How'd he look when you left?

BARBIE JO. I don't know, and right now, I don't care! I left him with Dave and the kids, but I swear that old hound actually looked smug this morning – frosting all over his muzzle. Thought he was pretty smart.

LOU. Well, smarter than Dave anyway.

BARBIE JO. That don't take a whole lot, Lou.

LOU. Don't I know it?

> *(The bell rings at the door as **SHARKY** and **PAULY**, looking very suspicious and checking to see if anyone sees them, come to the door and walk in. They start for a booth before **SHARKY** sees **DARLENE** and speaks.)*

SHARKY. Two coffees, doll.

DARLENE. Right away.

LOU. Hey, Darlene, aren't you forgetting something?

DARLENE. Cream and sugar?

LOU. Darlene, it's your wedding day! We're closed.

DARLENE. That's right. We're closed. I'm gettin' married!

LOU. Sorry fellas.

> (SHARKY *and* PAULY *have already made it to a booth.* SHARKY *slumps in the corner and hides behind a menu, looking nervous and watching the door.* PAULY *sits across from him and watches* DARLENE *with admiration.*)

SHARKY. *(Whispers to* PAULY.*)* We can't go out there now. They'll get us for sure!

> *(To* LOU.*)*

Just a cup of coffee. We'ze been driving all night. We'ze won't be no trouble.

PAULY. That's right. No trouble a'tall.

> *(To* DARLENE.*)*

Gosh, you're pretty.

DARLENE. Thanks. I'm getting married.

PAULY. You are?

DARLENE. Yep. We're going to the church just as soon as we put that cake back together. Barbie Jo – that's her in the kitchen. Say hi, Barbie Jo.

BARBIE JO. Hi fellas.

DARLENE. Barbie Jo's dog, Rufus, ate my cake. We're quick baking up a new one before anyone finds out.

PAULY. I had a dog once – Scar.

DARLENE. Cuz he had a scar?

PAULY. Nah, because my Uncle Guido gave him to me.

DARLENE. Oh, and he had a scar.

SHARKY. Guido was more the type to give 'em than to get 'em.

PAULY. I think it was more of a family name. Anyway, my dog, Scar ate a box of Ding Dongs one time. Wasn't never right after that. Spent hours tearing the fur out of his tail and barking at shadows

DARLENE. It's the chocolate. Not good for dogs. Now if he'd've eaten a box of Twinkies, he would've been fine!

LOU. Because Twinkies are so healthy.

BARBIE JO. Darlene, when you gonna stop carrying on about dogs and chocolate and help with this cake.

DARLENE. I can't do nothing 'til it comes out of the oven.

SHARKY. How 'bout dat coffee, Pauly?

PAULY. Oh right, boss.

> *(To* **DARLENE.***)*

Just one cup. Please? Then we'll be on our way.

DARLENE. Well sure. We got plenty of time. That cake has to bake another half hour at least, and then it has to cool.

> *(To* **LOU.***)*

No harm gettin' 'em one cup. Right, Lou?

LOU. It's your day, Darlene. If you want to spend it serving coffee, that's your prerogative.

> *(Sees* **DARLENE***'s quizzical look and explains.)*

Choice. That's your choice.

> *(Goes back into the kitchen to help* **BARBIE JO.***)*
>
> *(***DARLENE** *heads to the coffee urn, where she fills two cups as she speaks and returns to the table.)*

DARLENE. Lou's famous coffee. Two cups, pipin' hot. Where you fellas from?

PAULY. Jers...errr...

> *(About to speak when* **SHARKY** *jabs him sharply in the side.)*

Er... Jurassic...er... Jurassic Park.

DARLENE. Hey! I've heard of that! That's up north, right?

> *(***SHARKY** *shakes his head in disbelief.)*

PAULY. Yep. North Jurassic. Near the causeway.

SHARKY. You sure you're getting married today, doll?

DARLENE. Sure I'm sure. See my dress? People don't just walk around wearing wedding dresses if they ain't getting' married!

SHARKY. Just checking.

DARLENE. Why's that?

SHARKY. Cuz I never met a girl more perfectly suited for ol' Pauly here.

PAULY. *(Embarrassed.)* Sharky's just foolin'. He does that sometimes. So when's the wedding?

DARLENE. Three o'clock.

PAULY. I ain't been to a wedding in years. How 'bout you, boss? You like weddings?

SHARKY. Better than funerals. Don't nobody look good in black.

LOU. Not too many people look good in bridesmaid's dresses either.

PAULY. I like weddings.

DARLENE. If you boys'll be in town at three, you're welcome to come. Practically the whole town'll be there.

SHARKY. No. We couldn't possibly. We have somewhere we have to be. Ain't that right, Pauly?

PAULY. You sure, boss? Couldn't we stay? Just a while? I ain't been to a wedding in years.

SHARKY. You forgettin' why we came out here in the first place?

*(To **DARLENE**.)*

We couldn't possibly. Thanks all the same.

PAULY. *(Disappointed.)* Yeah. Thanks all the same.

SHARKY. Hey, doll, the coffee's good. You got Danish?

DARLENE. Best coffee in three states, and you should try some of Lou's world-famous pie when you have time. Hey, Lou, we got muffins or anything?

LOU. *(From kitchen.)* Check the walk-in, Darlene. There were some pastries left yesterday. Should still be there... unless Rufus found the key to my walk-in!

DARLENE. I'll check.

> *(To PAULY.)*

You too? Growing boy's gotta eat.

PAULY. If you got something. I don't wanna be no trouble.

DARLENE. No trouble at all.

> *(She turns and exits into kitchen.)*

SHARKY. *(Pulls PAULY down in the seat across from him.)* Don't get no ideas about that skirt! We're just laying low until we shake the Feds. Once they pass through, we can get back on the road.

PAULY. Don't worry, boss. I'm just bein' nice. It's her wedding day.

SHARKY. Well stop it! The last thing we need is for those girls to remember us and rat us out to the Feds. We need to blend in like anyone else. Just a pair of travelling salesman passing through. Got it?

PAULY. Got it. I forgot. I won't be nice no more.

SHARKY. Good! We get our coffee and Danish, and we get out. Nice and smooth. The boss's hideout's somewhere in these mountains. We'll disappear for a few weeks. The boss'll send for us when the heat's off.

PAULY. Nice and smooth.

SHARKY. Right! Nice and smooth. Cuz if anything goes wrong,

> *(He raises his coat to show a sidearm concealed underneath.)*

I'd hate to see little miss Dixie be late for her wedding.

PAULY. *(Horrified at the thought of DARLENE getting dragged into their plan.)* No, we don't want that. I won't be nice no more, Sharky. Honest.

DARLENE. *(Returns from kitchen bearing a tray filled with muffins and Danish.)* Try these! I bet they don't have nothing like this up in Jurassic Park!

SHARKY. I bet they don't neither.

PAULY. *(Takes a Danish and bites in.)* This is incredible!

DARLENE. I know! Lou's special recipe! She uses butter from a local dairy!

PAULY. You gotta try this, boss.

(Offers him the pastry he's just bitten.)

SHARKY. Not yours, you meathead! A fresh one!

PAULY. Oh, sorry.

DARLENE. *(Sets down the tray.)* Help yourselves, boys. These are day-old already.

PAULY. They're terrific!

SHARKY. What happened to no more Mr. Nice Guy?

PAULY. But, boss, you gotta try these!

SHARKY. Mmmm… Not bad.

BARBIE JO. Darlene, we got more trouble.

DARLENE. What's up, Barbie Jo?

BARBIE JO. I used the last of the yellow food coloring for the flowers on the cake yesterday. I can either use this red and make a nice pink, or you can have white flowers. Which do you want?

DARLENE. Will the pink ones taste like bubble gum

BARBIE JO. It's food coloring, Darlene. Not Double Bubble!

DARLENE. Jimmy likes bubble gum, but if it don't change the flavor none, I guess it doesn't matter. Surprise me!

BARBIE JO. Surprise you!

(To LOU.)

Surprise her! Haven't we had enough surprises for one day! What a wedding!

LOU. Nah, you want weddings? My cousin Floyd had a separate cake made out of chipped beef for his coon hounds. Wanted them to be part of the big day! Course,

Floyd likes his drink and after one too many toasts, he forgot which cake was which. When it was time to cut the cake, he fed chipped beef and Alpo to his new bride. Now that was a wedding!

BARBIE JO. Sad thing is, his bride, Luella, was such a bow wow, she didn't seem to notice!

LOU. It's true. That side of the family never did have good taste in women. Remember Cousin Beulah?

BARBIE JO. The one who filled up an entire booth by herself?

LOU. That's the one. Her husband took off huntin' one day about twelve years ago, and he ain't been heard from since. We figure he realized his mistake but didn't have the heart to tell her how he felt.

>   *(To **DARLENE**.)*

She eats when she's depressed, you know.

DARLENE. Jimmy wouldn't never do nothin' like that to me.

LOU. Of course not.

BARBIE JO. Funny how wedding stories always slide into break-up stories.

LOU. But that'll never happen with you and Jimmy! Barbie Jo, maybe you should check the cakes.

>   *(Cell phone rings. **BARBIE JO** fishes her phone out*
>   *of her apron and answers it.)*

BARBIE JO. Yep. Yep. Yep. Well, good for him.

>   *(Covers the phone with one hand and speaks to*
>   ***LOU** and **DARLENE**.)*

Rufus has been puking up yellow flowers all morning. That'll teach him!

>   *(Returns to her call.)*

Uh-huh. You're doing what? But why?

>   *(Sinks to a chair.)*

Oh my gosh… Who's with the kids? Mama… Wait, you left my mother with both kids and a puking dog? Oh, that's good. I'll never hear the end of this. Uh-huh. *You're* driving? Why?

(Pause.)

Oh, the monstrosity is better on rough roads and inclines. I keep forgetting. All I remember is the part where it's too big to fit in the garage and gets only four miles to the gallon! Dave, do I hear Bob Seger singing "Like a Rock." Turn that CD off and get down to business!

(Pause.)

No. I'll do it. Let me know when you have any news at all. I'll break it to Darlene. Should I finish the cake? I know *you* like cake, but that ain't exactly the issue here now is it, Dave?

(Pause.)

Fine. Call as soon as you find him. Uh-huh. Bye.

(Puts the phone away. Gangsters watch with keen interest.)

LOU. What now?

BARBIE JO. Darlene, honey, this may not be anything, but maybe you should sit down.

LOU. Oh God.

DARLENE. Sit down?

(Fluffs her skirt.)

I don't want to rumple my credenza.

BARBIE JO. Organza, Darlene! It's organza!

LOU. Barbie Jo…

BARBIE JO. That was Dave. Apparently he and Bill've been callin' Jimmy all morning. They wanted to know when they should pick him up to go to the church. When they got no answer, Bill drove out to Jimmy's place. He's gone, Darlene.

DARLENE. Gone?

BARBIE JO. Dave says it looks like cold feet. Just up and scampered off like a cotton tail facin' down a momma grizzly!

LOU. Are they sure? Maybe he just went out for a breath of fresh air.

BARBIE JO. On a hog farm!

DARLENE. Maybe he ran in to town for some last minute honeymoon necessities.

BARBIE JO. Like what? Garanimals?

DARLENE. Jimmy stopped wearing Garanimals when we got engaged, Barbie Jo!

BARBIE JO. They found a note, Darlene.

DARLENE. Gone?

BARBIE JO. Honey, it's okay. There's a lot better men out there than Jimmy Weaver!

DARLENE. Gone? Oh, Lou... How could he! *(Crying.)*

LOU. Now, Darlene, don't go getting' all worked up! Could be Dave heard it wrong or Bill read it wrong...

DARLENE. Or Jimmy got it wrong in the first place when he thought he wanted to marry me!

(Wails in a loud, unappealing manner.)

Oh, Lou!

SHARKY. She gonna be okay? That sound hurts my ears.

PAULY. Anything we'z can do to help?

SHARKY. Let's not go getting' involved.

BARBIE JO. *(To SHARKY.)* Heaven forbid!

LOU. *(To BARBIE JO.)* What are Bill and Dave doing now?

BARBIE JO. They're looking for him. Figure if they can find him, they can talk some sense to him.

DARLENE. I don't want him now! If he doesn't want me, I don't want him!

LOU. Now, Darlene, this happens all the time. Men are prone to panic at the last minute. Don't go gettin' hysterical on me.

(To **BARBIE JO.***)*

Where are they looking? There's a million places he could've gone to ground.

BARBIE JO. And only one place they figure Jimmy'd think no one else'll ever look.

LOU. The cabin?

BARBIE JO. The cabin.

DARLENE. *(Wails again.)* Oh, Lou! Even if they find him, they'll never get back in time!

(Lights fade.)

Scene Two

(Inside of a rough mountain cabin. Front door is upstage with a moose head hanging over it. A window on one side of the door shows trees just getting over a long winter. Cabin is furnished with an old sofa and coffee table and a chair and hassock off to one side. There is a bar with two bar stools to the right of the door, in front of the window upstage left. Another doorway leads to a hallway and bath upstage left. An old wood stove sits stage left of the couch. DAVE and BILL enter wearing tuxedos with orange hunting vests over them. DAVE wears a goofy hunting hat.)

DAVE. I don't get it. Why don't we just go find him?

BILL. We did find him.

DAVE. Don't feel like we found him. I don't see him. You see him?

BILL. No, but we saw his truck, so we know he's here. Probably wandering in the woods – thinkin' things over.

DAVE. And you're sure he'll come back to the cabin?

BILL. Of course he will. Where else would he go way up here?

DAVE. If he was smart, he'd high-tail it back to town and marry Darlene before her cousins get wind of this. That Fulmer clan ain't gonna take kindly to him jilting Darlene!

BILL. No one said he was jilting her!

DAVE. Read the note again.

BILL. *(Pulls rumpled paper out of his pocket and reads.)* "Darlene, please forgive me. I need to think, but I'm not sure marriage is right for me. I know you will understand. You are the most wonderful woman in the world. You deserve the best."

DAVE. At least he got that right! I don't know about you, but in my book, that's a jilt!

BILL. You just like saying that, don't you?

DAVE. Jilt, jilt, jilt. Kind of a funny word if you say it right, ain't it? Course never thought I'd ever be using it to describe Darlene. Do you think he means that last part about her deserving the best.

BILL. I hope so. If he really wants what's best for her, he'll come back to town with us and get married. We just have to find him.

DAVE. Considering the option means facing Darlene's cousins, I'd say that's definitely best.

> *(Looks around.)*

This place ain't changed a bit, has it?

BILL. Nope.

DAVE. You suppose anyone's been here since Christmas?

BILL. I doubt it.

DAVE. That was quite a night. Just two short months and look how things have changed.

> *(Door opens and* **JIMMY** *appears in jeans and a flannel shirt and coat.)*

JIMMY. Well I'll be! What are you two doing up here? And what in God's name are you wearing?

DAVE. What do you think we're wearing? These are the suits for your wedding, you moron. We wore the vests, just in case. Never can tell up in these mountains.

BILL. Course, won't be much of a wedding since Darlene seems to be missing something.

JIMMY. What's that?

DAVE & BILL. The groom!

JIMMY. Oh, you found my note, eh?

BILL. Yeah, we found the note. What's this about, Jimmy?

DAVE. Yeah, why'd you make us get all gussied up for a wedding you don't intend to have?

> *(Pulls at tie.)*

I hate these things. Always too tight.

BILL. The ties are adjustable, Dave. You can make it longer around the neck.

DAVE. They are? Why didn't no one ever tell me that?

JIMMY. I guess they enjoy seeing you choke yourself.

DAVE. I'm surrounded by comedians.

BILL. I know just how you feel.

JIMMY. Excuse me. Do you want to talk about Dave's tie or my wedding?

BILL. Dave's tie's easier, but you better tell us why you're here, lover boy.

JIMMY. Well, you know I love Darlene. She's the best thing that ever happened to me, but marriage... That's forever, you know.

DAVE. So I've heard.

BILL. So what's so bad about forever? Lotta guys would be happy to roll over and find Darlene in their bed every day for the rest of their lives.

DAVE. Wouldn't mind that myself.

JIMMY. Dave, get that picture right outta your head! Darlene's mine!

DAVE. Bill has a note that says otherwise.

BILL. Dave's right. Who wouldn't want to be married to Darlene? I mean, I love Lou, but...

DAVE. Kind of a nice thought though, ain't it?

JIMMY. 'Cept it might be a little crowded with Barbie Jo and your kids there too!

DAVE. Oh yeah... Plum forgot them, but Darlene...in the morning. All tousled and sleepy looking...

JIMMY. Now quit that!

DAVE. Quit what?

JIMMY. Thinkin' 'bout Darlene that way. She's practically my wife!

BILL. *(Shakes note in* **JIMMY***'s face.)* Oh yeah? Well not according to this, she ain't! You need to decide what you want, Jimmy. Everybody gets cold feet before a wedding. It's natural.

JIMMY. It is?

BILL. Why sure. Day I married Lou I thought of a thousand reasons to live, er...leave.

DAVE. Freudian slip, eh?

BILL. Yeah.

JIMMY. So why didn't ya?

BILL. Because there was that one really good reason to stay – Lou.

DAVE. Day I married Barbie Jo was the same thing.

JIMMY. It was?

DAVE. Sure.

JIMMY. And why'd you stay?

DAVE. Same reason. Lou.

BILL & JIMMY. What?

DAVE. Sure. I was scared to death; ready to rabbit just like you. Lou saw it in my eyes for sure, cuz she sat me down and reminded me of all the good times Barbie Jo and I'd had together and all the plans we'd made, and before I knew it, I was standing there watching Barbie Jo walk down the aisle looking like a princess in a fairy tale. I never felt happier or prouder than I did that day knowing she was taking me for her husband.

JIMMY. That's just it. I ain't sure I'm exactly husband material.

DAVE. *(Statement of truth.)* You're not.

BILL. We coulda told you that!

JIMMY. No, Bill, I mean it. What if I ain't good enough for Darlene? What if I do something stupid or foolish or... or...

BILL. Or normal for you?

JIMMY. Yeah!

BILL. You will.

JIMMY. Thanks for the vote of confidence!

BILL. I don't mean it that way. I mean, you're not perfect, but Darlene isn't asking you to be.

JIMMY. She ain't?

DAVE. She ain't?

BILL. She ain't. She knows you. She knows you like to sleep late and eat Frosted Flakes with Skittles every day.

JIMMY. Don't start in on my Frosted Flakes. They're an American institution!

DAVE. You're certifiable, you know! It's cereal!

 (Shaking his head.)

An American institution!

JIMMY. Everybody likes Frosted Flakes. I'm just man enough to admit it!

BILL. She knows you gamble once a week and flirt with pretty girls when you get the chance.

JIMMY. I can't help that. Just comes natural. Like breathin'.

DAVE. Don't worry. She'll break you of that soon enough.

BILL. She knows you can't cook to save your life and you won't lift a finger to clean the house.

DAVE. You sure we want to talk him into marrying her?

BILL. Why?

DAVE. We'd be doing Darlene a favor if we took him to the state line and sent him on his way.

JIMMY. Hey!

BILL. But that's just it, ain't it? Despite everything – despite the fact Jimmy ain't no prize...

JIMMY. Thanks again, Bill

BILL. ...Darlene loves him. She's not trying to change him. She's not asking for more than he's willing to give. She's asking him to share his love and his life. You do love her, don't you?

DAVE. If you don't, I know fourteen Fulmer cousins who left their stills to come to the wedding today who're gonna be awfully unhappy with you.

JIMMY. Course I love Darlene! How could I not! Why, she's the kindest, prettiest, sweetest girl anywhere! Darlene has a heart of gold and the face of a centerfold. Who wouldn't want that! Have you ever seen her be grumpy or cross or even unhappy? She just floats around on a cloud of sweetness.

DAVE. Oh yeah, he's in love.

JIMMY. She's the most beautiful woman in the world.

DAVE. Yeah, they all do that.

JIMMY. Do what?

DAVE. Look fabulous just before the wedding. It's like they glow or something. Reminds me of a duck call.

BILL. Dave, you have got to be the strangest person I know. How on earth does a pretty girl like Darlene remind you of a duck call?

DAVE. She uses her looks like a hunter uses his call. It lures the victim in and seals his fate.

JIMMY. Darlene don't go for no huntin'. Besides, I'm the lucky one for baggin' her.

DAVE. Then what're you doin' up here three hours before your wedding?

JIMMY. Marrying Darlene would make me the luckiest man alive.

BILL. Well, now you're talkin' sense.

JIMMY. But that's the problem.

DAVE. Being the luckiest man alive's a problem?

JIMMY. I don't deserve her.

DAVE. *(Kicks* **JIMMY** *in the rear end.)* Here's something you do deserve! Feel better?

JIMMY. No! Yes! You know what I mean. Darlene's just… she's just, I dunno. She's special.

BILL. *(Ironic.)* You can say that again.

JIMMY. Guys go out of their way to do stuff for her, and not just young guys. I mean everyone from the five-year-olds in her Sunday school class to the old men at her grandma's nursing home. Everywhere we go, men look at Darlene and melt. How do I compete with that?

DAVE. Compete with what?

BILL. Competition's over. In case no one told you, you won.

JIMMY. But how do I know there isn't someone better for her out there?

BILL. You don't. This time, you trust Darlene.

DAVE. Well, no offense, but Darlene ain't the sharpest pencil in the box. Maybe Jimmy's right.

BILL. You ain't helping, Dave!

JIMMY. You take that back! Darlene don't come across as smart, but she knows things! And people! She really knows people. And I never knew anyone who knew more about animals! Why, she's taken to my hogs like a duck to water.

DAVE. Yeah, but have you explained to her yet how them hogs actually become the bacon Lou serves at the diner?

JIMMY. Baby steps, Dave. Baby steps.

BILL. Listen, we don't have all day. Right now, Darlene's back in town thinkin' the wedding's off.

JIMMY. She knows?

DAVE. I called Barbie Jo.

BILL. If you want to work this out, we have to get back. Now.

JIMMY. So what do I do when all those guys look at me like they want to take my place?

BILL. You smile and nod and drop an arm around your girl and let them know "That ship has sailed." You'll get used to handling it. Men with beautiful wives always do, ain't that right, Dave.

DAVE. Why you askin' me?

BILL. *(Smacks him.)* Cut that out.

DAVE. Oh Barbie Jo!

(To **JIMMY.***)*

Sure, you get used to it, and then the kids come along, and she gets fat and cranky, and her mother makes you crazy and she stops baking your favorite cookies cuz she's always too busy and...

BILL. Dave.

DAVE. What?

BILL. Give it a rest. You've helped enough for one day. Call Barbie Jo and tell her we're bringin' Jimmy in. Right, Jim?

JIMMY. Won't hurt to try. I mean, how bad can it be?

BILL. That's the spirit!

DAVE. *(Takes out cell phone, presses a button, and looks at it.)* Just one thing, Bill.

BILL. What's that?

DAVE. Seems you forgot how it was at Christmas, but there ain't no cell service up here. We'll have to call the girls when we get closer to town.

BILL. Greatest single invention since the wheel, and it never works when you need it. Come on, saddle up. We got a wedding to get to.

> *(**BILL** turns and opens the front door. **DAVE** starts to follow and notices **JIMMY** starting to skulk away toward the bathroom door. **DAVE** grabs **JIMMY** and shoves him out the front door. Lights fade.)*

Scene Three

(Back inside Lou's Diner. **LOU** *and* **BARBIE JO** *stand next to* **DARLENE,** *who sits at a table in the center of the diner. She has a tissue box in her lap and a pile of soggy, crumpled tissues on the table next to her. She still wears her wedding gown, but she is a wretched, sobbing mess.* **PAULY** *and* **SHARKY** *sit quietly, watching the scene unfold.)*

DARLENE. Jilted, Lou! Me! Darlene Fulmer, jilted! G-I-L-T-E-D! Jilted!

BARBIE JO. You know, that's a funny word if you say it right.

LOU. *(Scolds.)* Barbie Jo!

(To **DARLENE.***)*

Darlene, honey, he didn't jilt you. He's just having second thoughts. That's all. It happens all the time.

DARLENE. It does?

LOU. Why sure it does. You know how men are. No matter how good they have it, they can't stand the thought of giving up their freedom.

BARBIE JO. That's true. Think they'll be spending the rest of their life in some sort of purgatory.

DARLENE. Is that what he thinks? Jimmy thinks life with me will be purgatory?!

LOU. Of course not!

PAULY. How could life with you be anything but heaven?

DARLENE. Ain't you just the sweetest thing, Pauly. Lou, what's purgatory?

LOU. Honey, let's not worry about it now. Let's get you cleaned up and dried off.

DARLENE. I don't see why. Ain't gonna be no wedding. Oh my gosh, did anyone call Lester?

SHARKY. *(Despite his hard shell, he's been pulled in.)* Who's Lester?

BARBIE JO. Lester's Darlene's third cousin twice removed and the minister who's officiating the wedding.

DARLENE. *(Wails.)* Except there ain't gonna be a wedding!

LOU. Now, Darlene, we don't know that. Why Dave and Bill probably found Jimmy hours ago. They're probably getting him dressed and ready even as we speak.

DARLENE. Then why haven't they called.

BARBIE JO. You know Dave always forgets his cell phone. Even if it's with him, he forgets to use it.

LOU. Yet he can remember every specification of that hemi dual cab extended length pickup thing he drives.

BARBIE JO. Surely, you ain't expectin' me to make sense of Dave!

LOU. Don't expect that of anyone, Barbie Jo.

DARLENE. Bill has a phone.

LOU. Bill's probably too busy helping Jimmy to call. Let's not bother Lester until we know exactly what's going on, okay?

PAULY. *(Sniffs.)* You smell something, boss?

SHARKY. Nah, why? You hungry again?

PAULY. Like something burning…

> *(Smoke wafts through the kitchen window and into the diner.)*

BARBIE JO. Smoke! My cake!

> *(Rises and rushes into the kitchen.)*

LOU. Not this again!

DARLENE. My cake!

BARBIE JO. I forgot all about it, what with the jilting and all.

> *(Fans at the smoke.)*

DARLENE. See, Lou!

> *(Wails.)*

Jilted! G-I-L…

BARBIE JO. Stop spellin' it, Darlene. You're makin' me crazy!

DARLENE. I can never show my face again!

(*Wails.*)

LOU. Thanks a lot, Barbie Jo. I just had her calmed down!

PAULY. Is it dangerous? The fire?

LOU. The smoke? Not for you fellas. You ain't stayin'. Remember?

SHARKY. Not the smoke. The fire. Will it bring the cops?

LOU. Nah, they're all at the church for the wedding. Besides this happens a lot.

PAULY. It does?

LOU. Let's just say Barbie Jo has problems baking under pressure.

BARBIE JO. That's not fair! I had everything under control until Jimmy jilted Darlene.

DARLENE. Oh, Loooooouuuuuu!

LOU. Barbie Jo, please! Enough with the "J" word!

DARLENE. (*Truly mystified.*) J?

PAULY. It don't seem possible anyone could jilt you, Darlene. You being so nice and all.

(**DARLENE** *cries harder.*)

LOU. I know you're trying to help, Pauly, but it might be best if I take care of Darlene.

PAULY. Oh, sure. Sorry. I just want to cheer her up.

LOU. The best way to cheer her up now is to get that cake back on track.

PAULY. We can do that. Can't we, boss? Didn't you used to bake?

SHARKY. Not me personally, but my grandmother from Sicily, Maria Louisa –

(*Stops and crosses himself.* **PAULY** *follows suit.*)

God rest her soul, was a baker's daughter.

PAULY. Let's help, boss. Dese dames need us.

SHARKY. Why should we get involved?

PAULY. Cuz Darlene's our friend. Come on, boss. It's a chance to do some good for a change. Let's help out. Whadya say?

SHARKY. *(To himself.)* I know I'm gonna regret dis.

> *(To* **BARBIE JO**.*)*

You'z need a hand in the kitchen, Barbie Jo? Pauly and I can whip up the best cake you ever ate.

BARBIE JO. Really? Because this mess is gonna keep me busy a while.

DARLENE. You'd do that for me? But you don't even know me.

PAULY. Sure we do. Don't we, boss?

SHARKY. Sure we do. You helped us when we needed a place to hideout...er, I mean, when we needed a place to rest. You're already having a crummy day. Besides, I ain't baked in years! Might be fun!

BARBIE JO. Fun, he says...

SHARKY. You ever baked, Pauly?

PAULY. No, boss, but I can help. Tell me what to do.

SHARKY. *(Stands and heads to the kitchen.)* See! It's settled! Pauly and I'll start on the cake batter while Barbie Jo cleans up.

DARLENE. You think it'll be okay, Lou?

LOU. It couldn't hurt. You boys need anything special?

SHARKY. You got more of dem aprons? I don't wanna mess up the suit.

LOU. Sure. In back. Barbie Jo'll show you.

SHARKY. Oh, and...

> *(Leans and whispers into* **LOU**'s *ear as he passes by the table where* **DARLENE** *sits. He's asking her for a special, secret ingredient for the cake. Stands up and continues.)*

Can you get that here?

LOU. I'll make a few calls. If they know it's for Darlene's wedding cake, I'm sure we'll be able to lay our hands on some.

BARBIE JO. What do they need?

LOU. Never mind. I'll call Dalton and see if he can find it. If not, he might be able to get what we need from Darlene's Uncle Jedediah.

BARBIE JO. But Jedediah's the biggest moonshiner in four counties.

> *(Understands.)*

Ohhhhhh.

DARLENE. Thank you! You're all so nice. Especially considering there may not even be a wedding.

LOU. Now, Darlene, quit talkin' that way. You know Jimmy loves you.

DARLENE. Well, I thought he did.

LOU. Does. He loves you. Present tense. Dave and Bill just need to remind him how much.

DARLENE. But why, Lou? Why can't he be as excited about the wedding as I am?

LOU. Honey, ain't never no one as excited about anything as you are, and that's the truth!

DARLENE. You know what I mean.

LOU. I do. Honestly, I think he's worried he'll disappoint you.

DARLENE. He could never disappoint me, Lou. I love him.

BARBIE JO. He's a man. Give him time.

LOU. *(Ignores BARBIE JO's comment.)* I know you do, Darlene, but Jimmy hasn't always been a paragon of virtue.

DARLENE. *(Pretending she understands.)* No, of course not.

> *(Puzzled.)*

Why, should he be?

LOU. *(Realizes she is using words much too large for DARLENE to comprehend.)* What I'm sayin' is, for a while there he was nothin' more than a good for nothin', dirty, skirt chasing mongrel.

DARLENE. *(Gets it.)* Oh that! Well, he's over that.

LOU. I know it, and you know it, but does Jimmy know it?

DARLENE. Gee, I hope so.

LOU. He's been a model fiancé since Christmas, but what if he's worried he might slip.

DARLENE. Slip?

LOU. You know, maybe stray to greener pastures.

DARLENE. Are there greener pastures?

LOU. Honey, don't go asking me to explain Jimmy Weaver. All's I know is he loves you, and don't ask me why, but I got a feeling, he's comin' back.

DARLENE. You do?

BARBIE JO. Lou, what should I do with these burned cakes? Put 'em out for the birds?

LOU. Throw 'em out, Barbie Jo.

DARLENE. Wait, Lou, isn't there traditionally a groom's cake? You know, special like, just for the groom and his men?

LOU. Yeah.

DARLENE. Well, in that case, I have an idea for one of those cakes.

> *(To **BARBIE JO**.)*

Barbie Jo, do me a favor. Ice the smallest of the burnt cakes and set it aside. If Lou's right, and Jimmy comes back, I don't want him getting' off scot-free.

BARBIE JO. You know, Darlene, there's hope for you yet.

DARLENE. There is?

BARBIE JO. Yep. You're getting over being a girlfriend and starting to think like a wife!

> *(Bell rings as the door opens and **LESTER** enters wearing a nice suit and carrying a large Bible.)*

LESTER. Darlene, what on earth are you girls doing here? I expected you at the church an hour ago!

*(Crosses to **DARLENE**, sees the tears, and crouches down to look at her face.)*

What happened?

(She hugs him.)

DARLENE. Oh, Lester...

LOU. Morning, Lester. We're having a bit too much excitement this morning.

LESTER. So nothin' serious then?

LOU. I don't think so. Dave's ol' dog, Rufus, ate the top tiers off the wedding cake, so we came in to bake up replacements.

LESTER. She's cryin' like that over cake?

DARLENE. No. Jimmy left me! I've been jilted! G-I-L-T-E-D.

BARBIE JO. Darlene, honey, stop spellin'. It's not your best subject.

LESTER. Jimmy did what?

DARLENE. Dave and Bill couldn't find him this mornin', so Bill drove out to the farm, and Jimmy was gone. He left a note.

LESTER. Dear God. I hope the cousins don't find out.

LOU. Bill and Dave think they know where he went. They're out after him now.

LESTER. And you think he'll come back?

LOU. I do. I never seen a man more in love with Darlene.

LESTER. There have been more than a passing few.

LOU. Ain't that the truth! But this ain't like that, Lester. You've seen how they are together. He just needs some calmin' down.

LESTER. I have seen how they are together, but that don't mean he can't be spooked.

LOU. That's all I think it is. He's spooked. Bill and Dave'll find him and talk some sense to him, and he'll be back here before anyone else has to know anything ever happened.

LESTER. Well, I hate to see all those people who came for the wedding be disappointed, and you know how Darlene's cousins get when they come to town. I don't need that headache on top of everything else.

DARLENE. Everything else?

LESTER. Dalton called about an hour ago. We got an APB on a coupla bad guys might be passin' through. I'm hopin' it don't amount to nothin', but if I get a call, I may have to put on my sheriff's hat today.

SHARKY. *(In kitchen, he has not heard* **LESTER**.*)* Barbie Jo, where's dat whisk?

BARBIE JO. Look behind you.

SHARKY. *Grazie!*

LOU. That reminds me. Dalton gonna make it for the service?

LESTER. Nah, I have to leave one deputy on the desk. Just in case…

LOU. You're a great sheriff, Lester, but I've always liked you better as a minister.

LESTER. Lot of people can't see the two in one person, but I always felt it was just two sides of the same coin.

> *(Pause.)*

New help in the kitchen?

LOU. *(Absently.)* Friends of Darlene's.

LESTER. No one makes friends like our Darlene.

LOU. Ain't that the truth?

DARLENE. Lester, have you ever used your sheriff's privileges to retrieve a runaway groom?

LESTER. Now, Darlene, honey, if Jimmy don't have sense enough to come back on his own, I ain't sure he deserves you. Let's just wait and see things work out.

> *(Pause.)*

Why don't you run to the lady's room and splash some water on your face. You'll feel a whole lot better.

DARLENE. Maybe you're right. Sittin' here cryin' ain't doin' me any good. I must look a fright!

> *(Rises and walks wobbly to the restroom door and exits.)*

LESTER. Sweet kid.

> *(Shakes his head in disbelief.)*

Jilted. Who would've ever thought it? You girls gonna tell her she's spellin' it wrong?

LOU. Barbie Jo's just itchin' to set her straight, but I don't see the point.

LESTER. And what about Jimmy?

LOU. Nope, he can't spell either.

LESTER. Well, there's that, but I meant where do you think he is?

LOU. Oh, Bill thinks he may be hiding at the Christmas cabin.

LESTER. And they went up there to find him? That ain't exactly the safest road this time of year. Lots of mud and washouts.

LOU. I know, Lester. I'm hoping all this quiet is just bad cell phone reception in them mountains. We haven't heard a peep.

LESTER. Well, this might be a good time for me to set aside the badge and pick up the collar.

LOU. What do you mean?

LESTER. Only thing we can do now is pray.

> *(They solemnly join hands as lights fade. End Act I.)*

ACT II

Scene One

(Lights come up on the empty cabin. Suddenly the front door bursts open, and DAVE *falls through. He is covered with mud. This can be effectively shown without ruining the tux coats by smearing mud on the hunting vests, faces, and hands of the men. Best idea is to have two sets of hunting vests: one clean for Act I and one pre-dirtied for Act II.* BILL *and* JIMMY *follow* DAVE *in, both looking as dirty and dingy as* DAVE.*)*

JIMMY. Who would've thought there'd be that much mud up here this time of year?

BILL. You ever up here in the spring before?

JIMMY. Nope. I only come for deer season.

DAVE. Ever heard of the Saint Valentine's Day mudslide?

JIMMY. Maybe. I usually have other things to do on Valentine's Day.

BILL. Half the mountain slid into the next town. Fortunately, most folks knew it was coming. Heavy run-off that year. Not many casualties, but lots of damage.

DAVE. Casualties?

(Panic.)

You think this mountain's gonna slide?

BILL. This mountain ain't goin' nowhere.

DAVE. Why not? You said...

BILL. That was different. It ain't been raining yet this year. This is mostly just mud from the early thaw.

DAVE. Well, that's a relief.

JIMMY. But if the trucks're stuck in the mud, how we gonna get home? My wedding's in two hours!

DAVE. Let's just be clear. My truck is not stuck! Your truck is stuck. I just can't get my truck around your truck! I've got an eight valve, dual quad core, super turbo charged hemi. I can get outta anything! Your wimpy little farm boy truck's the reason we can't get home! You're blockin' the whole road!

JIMMY. Well, I don't see your truck doin' no better!

DAVE. It could if your truck got outta the way!

JIMMY. I didn't know the roads were nothin' but mud! You think I planned this!

DAVE. Well, the truck was here when we pulled up. That's how we knew we'd found you. Why'd you move it?

JIMMY. I wanted to be ready to run in case you tried to take me back.

BILL. Ain't nobody goin' back now.

DAVE. You did this on purpose!

BILL. Hey, hey now. Let's just calm down. Gettin' riled up ain't doin' us a bit of good. We need to think.

DAVE. Those of us equipped for the task.

JIMMY. You callin' me stupid?

DAVE. This ain't the first time you got us stuck up here!

JIMMY. Seems it was your fault last time!

DAVE. Yeah?

JIMMY. Yeah!

DAVE. You're the one who left the key in the ignition.

JIMMY. Well, you're the one who didn't ask for the key!

BILL. Enough.

> *(To **DAVE**.)*

You. Stand there.

> *(To **JIMMY**.)*

You. Over here. Stop fighting each other. We need to find a way outta here.

DAVE. If we get Jimmy's toy truck outta the way, my hemi half ton four by four'll make it through that mud like nobody's business.

JIMMY. Hey!

BILL. No offense, Jimmy, but that's what I was thinkin'.

JIMMY. Hey!

BILL. Not the toy part. It's just Dave's truck's made for this terrain.

DAVE. *(Gloats.)* See?

JIMMY. Cuz he's always high-tailin' it to the mountains to get away from Barbie Jo and the kids.

BILL. Let's not start that again.

DAVE. You're just jealous my truck's bigger than yours!

JIMMY. Oh yeah?

DAVE. Yeah!

JIMMY. Well my truck's better at maneuvering than yours.

DAVE. Who cares? My truck don't need to maneuver. I drive over anything that gets in my way!

BILL. Do you think you can make a path around Jimmy's truck through the woods?

DAVE. Did you see how steep that hill is, Bill? I ain't interested in rollin' my pride and joy down the side of that mountain.

JIMMY. See! If it weren't so big and bulky, you might be able to squeeze in next to me on the road.

DAVE. I'm warning you, Jimmy! I ain't about to risk my neck just so's you can get married.

JIMMY. *(Shocked at himself.)* I really want to.

BILL. Want to what?

JIMMY. When Dave just said that, I realized… I really want to be married to Darlene. I didn't think I wanted marriage, but now that we're stuck here and might not make it back, I realize that's all I really want!

DAVE. That's human nature. Wantin' what you don't have.

JIMMY. So what's the secret?

BILL. Secret to what?

JIMMY. You know…happiness. If all we want's what we don't have, how can we ever be happy? We'll always be chasin' after what's not ours.

DAVE. Seriously! We're stuck in the mountains, covered with mud, about to miss your wedding, which by the way'll put us in trouble so deep with our wives, we may as well just stay here forever, and you want the secret to happiness?

JIMMY. Well, yeah… Don't you?

DAVE. I don't know. Never really thought about it.

> *(To* **BILL.***)*

What'd'ya got, Bill?

BILL. I don't suppose I got much t'all. But if you're askin', I'd have to say happy people choose to be happy every day.

JIMMY. Wait, you're sayin' the secret to happiness is just choose to be happy? That's it? Just like that?

DAVE. *(Sarcastic.)* Just like that!

BILL. Pretty much. Y'see with Internet and cell phones and twittering tweets all over the place, it's gotten so a man can't hardly avoid a constant stream of news, and I don't mind sayin', most seems pretty bad and gettin' worse every day.

DAVE. Ain't that the truth!

BILL. Happy people avoid that stuff. They wake up in the morning and thank the good Lord for another day with their family, their friends, and for having a purpose in life.

JIMMY. So avoidin' the news'll make me happy?

DAVE. Can't hurt!

BILL. Not just that. I mean you can't avoid it entirely, but you can be careful about what you let in here…

> *(Taps his head.)*

And here.

(Taps his heart.)

What gets in becomes part of who you are. Bein' happy is the choice to get up and find something good in all the craziness of life when everyone around you's focusing on the bad.

DAVE. You think it's that easy?

BILL. I didn't say it was easy. I said it's a choice.

JIMMY. So when I woke up this morning in a panic about gettin' married, I was choosing to see the bad…the boredom, the responsibility, the bills.

DAVE. The in-laws!

BILL. That's right. You could have chosen to think about all the great things God is givin' you by givin' you Darlene as your wife.

JIMMY. Like the way she sings to the cats in the barn when she's puttin' out their food at night, and how she hugs everyone she knows whether they like it or not…

DAVE. Or how she looks in a mini skirt and heels!

JIMMY. *(Tries to punch DAVE, but BILL steps in and stops him.)* I warned you about that!

DAVE. Just tryin' to help!

BILL. Listen, I got an idea that might just get us outta here, but you two knuckleheads are gonna have to work together for a change. No more fightin', no more teasin', no more squabblin'. Think you can do it?

JIMMY. Will it get me to the church on time?

BILL. I think so.

JIMMY. And no more cracks about Darlene's legs?

DAVE. Cross my heart.

JIMMY. Then what have we got to lose? Let's go! My tux is on the bed, I can change and get to Darlene in plenty of time!

(He turns and practically runs out the cabin door.)

Come on, fellas. I got a wedding to go to!

DAVE. If I didn't know better, I'd swear that boy looks excited about getting married!

BILL. Don't worry, Dave. He just chose to be happy! Let's make our own choice and be excited with him.

DAVE. Well, that's right, dad gum. We're gonna get that boy home so he can marry Darlene, and I'm gonna kiss Barbie Jo full on the mouth in front of God and everybody!

BILL. That's the spirit, Dave!

(Claps him on the back.)

Let's go!

(They turn with a spring in their step and follow **JIMMY** *out the door. Lights fade.)*

Scene Two

*(Back at the diner, the girls are putting the finishing touches on the wedding cake as **PAULY** and **SHARKY** look on proudly. The men still wear their aprons.)*

PAULY. *(Slurs a bit.)* How much time we got, Lou?

LOU. *(Checks her watch.)* Fifteen minutes. Tops. If we aren't outta here in fifteen, we won't make it.

BARBIE JO. You boys drinking that hooch Dalton brought over from Darlene's uncle?

PAULY. The boss said we should taste it since it wasn't exactly the same stuff his grandmother used.

(Crosses himself.)

God rest her soul.

BARBIE JO. How many *tastes* did you have?

SHARKY. Enough to be sure this'll be the best wedding cake ever.

BARBIE JO. Lou, they're smashed. Maybe we should taste the cake before we go.

LOU. There's no time!

SHARKY. I guarantee you's gonna love this cake. Grandma Crionelli's cakes was world-famous!

*(**BARBIE JO** starts to put the bride and groom on top.)*

BARBIE JO. The new groom isn't an exact match, but it was the best we could find on short notice.

(It would be fun if the new groom for the top of the cake was a Minion or G.I. Joe or X-Man or something else that will amuse the audience.)

LOU. Why don't we just wait on those. Don't want to jinx it.

DARLENE. Who cares about the cake if there's no groom?

LOU. Relax, honey. You got yourself a groom.

DARLENE. But we still don't know if Jimmy's even gonna show up.

SHARKY. I ain't had this much fun in years! I should bake more often!

PAULY. It's very relaxing. Therapeutic.

BARBIE JO. Jimmy'll show. If he don't, Dave better have a darn good explanation.

PAULY. Darlene, sometimes, you just gotta believe.

> *(The girls stop what they're doing and look at* **PAULY** *in shock.)*

What? Cuz I'm a big, tough guy, I can't have feelings?

LOU. Of course you can, and Pauly's right! We just gotta have faith Bill and Dave found him and took him straight to the church.

DARLENE. But what if they didn't? What if…

SHARKY. One thing I've learned over the years, Darlene, you can "what if" yourself to death. What if I hadn't knocked over that liquor store with my cousin Vinny when I was twelve? What if I hadn't bought dem brass knuckles when I was fourteen? What if I never got into collections with Uncle Guido? You can make yourself crazy with "what if." Lou's right! Have a little faith!

LOU. See!

SHARKY. *(Raises a flask.)* Want a drink? I never had nothin' like it.

BARBIE JO. I think you've had enough.

> *(To* **DARLENE**.*)*

Get them some coffee.

> *(To* **SHARKY**.*)*

What is it you do again, Mr. Sharky? I don't think I caught your line of work.

SHARKY. We's in…uh, commodities.

PAULY. That's right, commodities! *(Chuckles.)*

SHARKY. And banking and a bit of collections.

DARLENE. Collections! You collect?

SHARKY. Sure, when we's forced to.

DARLENE. I collect too! My biggest collection is thimbles. I have 'em from forty-three states and two countries.

BARBIE JO. I keep tellin' you, Darlene, Alaska ain't a country.

DARLENE. Barbie Jo, I watch *White Christmas* every year on TV, and that Rosemary Clooney says her brother's out of the country in Alaska every time. I figure she should know where her own brother is!

BARBIE JO. And that's why you failed geography in high school.

DARLENE. Who says I failed geography, Barbie Jo? I got an "A" in that class!

BARBIE JO. Geography? You got an "A" from mean old Mr. Appleton?

DARLENE. Mr. Appleton liked my end of year presentation.

BARBIE JO. The one on markets and monetary influences of a single commodity in a specific foreign country?

DARLENE. Yep, I had Brazil. Did you know they sell the tiniest swimsuits you ever saw there?

PAULY. *(Gulps.)* They do?

DARLENE. They sure do. Mr. Appleton said he'd never seen nothin' like it!

BARBIE JO. I bet not! Well, that explains the "A" then, don't it?

LOU. Darlene just lives under a different set of rules than the rest of us, Barbie Jo. You can either fight it or accept it, but it ain't gonna change.

PAULY. I'd've given you an "A" too, Darlene.

DARLENE. Thank you, Pauly.

> *(Sigh.)*

I guess you're right, Lou. I just need to have faith Jimmy'll show up. And if he doesn't...

BARBIE JO. If he doesn't, Dave better plan to sleep with old Rufus for a month!

LOU. It's more than that, Darlene. It's about having faith in people even when they've let you down, because you know they have that voice inside of 'em tellin' 'em to do the right thing.

DARLENE. Like my little voice?

BARBIE JO. Not exactly. Your little voice is a whole different thing.

LOU. Now, Barbie Jo, we don't know. Maybe that little voice Darlene listens to is her moral compass, her spirit guide, her higher power. It could be exactly the same thing.

SHARKY. In the Catholic church, we call that God.

(**PAULY** *makes the sign of the cross.*)

LOU. We do too. I just don't like to be preachy.

BARBIE JO. Since when?

LOU. (*To* **DARLENE.**) That voice inside'll bring Jimmy back when he heads in the wrong direction.

DARLENE. It will?

BARBIE JO. Seems to work with Dave, and he's had lots of practice!

LOU. Sure. Jimmy won't ever be perfect.

BARBIE JO. He sure proved that.

LOU. And, he's gonna make mistakes again.

BARBIE JO. And again…

LOU. Hopefully nothing dumb as this, but…

BARBIE JO. But you should probably expect it.

LOU. She's right. You should. What I'm sayin' is, sometimes we gotta have faith in what's in a person's heart.

SHARKY. Lou, I hope you don't mind me sayin', you're one of the smartest broads I ever seen. What you say makes a lot of sense.

(*Swallows from flask again.* **LOU** *tries to replace the flask with a coffee cup.*)

LOU. Thank you. I think.

PAULY. Wow! The boss don't normally have nothin' good to say about broads...er dames. I mean, ladies. Says they got no common sense at all.

BARBIE JO. Well, I don't know about women where you're from, but here in the country, women pride themselves on common sense. Even Darlene, who ain't got a bit of horse sense has plenty of common sense.

SHARKY. I see that. She's a veritable paragon.

(DARLENE *looks confused and turns to* LOU.)

LOU. Don't stress yourself, honey. It's a good thing.

DARLENE. Oh, okay.

LOU. We need to get this cake packed up and over to the church, but Darlene, just remember, marriage ain't easy. This today...the wedding. This is the easy part. Everything after takes work to succeed, and part of that work is having faith in your partner to do the right thing when the chips are down.

DARLENE. And you think Jimmy's gonna do the right thing? You think he's comin' back to marry me.

LOU. I'd bet my top secret, award-winning pie recipe on it!

DARLENE. Really? You would? Really, Lou?

LOU. (*Hugs her.*) Really. Now, you just sit here quiet while we get this thing loaded. Don't want you gettin' frosting on your dress.

(*They roll the table the cake is on toward the kitchen.*)

DARLENE. But why don't they call.

LOU. Maybe they're busy.

BARBIE JO. Or outta range.

SHARKY. Or they was unavoidably detained. We sees it all the time.

PAULY. Or they forgot.

DARLENE. Forgot my wedding! Give me that.

(Takes **SHARKY***'s flask before anyone can stop her and drinks. Coughs and gags.)*

LOU. Darlene! Stop that. Moonshine is not the answer!

PAULY. It's not!

SHARKY. Then she needs a different question.

BARBIE JO. You sure you boys can carry the cake? Last thing we need is an accident now.

SHARKY. Nah. We're fine. I never felt so alive, like all my senses are on fire!

LOU. You boys ever had mountain shine before.

BARBIE JO. It's a little stronger than your average liqueur.

PAULY. We'z can hold our booze. Right, boss?

BARBIE JO. That's what everybody says the first time. Maybe we should take them back to the house.

LOU. Your house? Your mother's there with two kids and a puking dog.

BARBIE JO. How about your house?

SHARKY. No, we'z going to the wedding.

BARBIE JO. You ready to meet Darlene's country cousins?

PAULY. I wanna meet Jimmy. He better be good enough for our Darlene.

SHARKY. We made the cake. We'z going to see everyone enjoy it.

PAULY. If he don't come back and marry Darlene, we can teach him a lesson too.

(To **DARLENE***.)*

If things don't work out with Jimmy, you wanna see a movie this week?

SHARKY. You like it here, don't'cha Pauly?

PAULY. I do. It smells good. Clean. It's kinda nice, ain't it boss?

SHARKY. Yeah, I could see opening a franchise here. Not right away, of course. We need to finish our vacation first. Remember.

PAULY. Vacation?

(**SHARKY** *pokes him again.*)

Oh, yeah. I almost forgot. You's girls know where there's a cabin in these mountains.

BARBIE JO. There's lots of cabins in these mountains. Lou's husband, Bill, is a guide. He knows all of 'em.

LOU. Bill'll be happy to help you boys find your cabin – after Darlene and Jimmy get hitched. First things first.

SHARKY. We'd appreciate it.

PAULY. We have orders to lay low 'til the heat's off.

SHARKY. *(Tries to cover.)* 'Til it warms up. He means I'm supposed to take it easy 'til it warms up. The cold weather ain't good for my lumbago.

PAULY. Uh, yeah. His lumbago.

SHARKY. Doctor's orders.

> (**LOU** *and* **BARBIE JO** *exchange a knowing glance while* **DARLENE** *fusses with her hair and makeup in a hand mirror.*)

LOU. We'll introduce you to Dave and Bill before the ceremony.

BARBIE JO. And Lester.

LOU. And Lester.

SHARKY. Friend of yours?

LOU. Darlene's minister, remember? He sometimes helps Bill when a job requires extra manpower.

SHARKY. We won't need more manpower. We just need to be pointed in the right direction.

LOU. Oh, I think Lester may want to come along. I have a feeling he's gonna take a shine to you boys.

BARBIE JO. I think you're right. Lester's sure to be interested in Darlene's new friends from outta town.

SHARKY. You sure you don't mind us taggin' along?

PAULY. Yeah, we's don't wanna be no trouble.

LOU. *(Surveys the wedding cake.)* The cake looks great! We couldn't have done it without you. It's only right you come to the church. But no trouble. Promise me. If

Jimmy isn't there, you boys just head on out and find your cabin. Deal?

SHARKY. *(Shakes* **LOU***'s hand.)* Deal!

DARLENE. Why I won't take "no" for an answer! You just have to come to my wedding! People will be talkin' about it for months.

BARBIE JO. Talkin' 'bout what, Darlene?

DARLENE. That Jimmy and I had guests who came all the way from Jurassic Park!

BARBIE JO. Darlene, you do know…?

LOU. Give it a rest, Barbie Jo. It's her day. Let's get the van and get this cake loaded up.

> *(Quietly aside to* **BARBIE JO***.)*

You're gonna have to keep them busy when we get there. I'll need a minute to talk to Lester alone.

BARBIE JO. Tell me again why we talked her out of eloping.

LOU. Ready, boys? One, two, three…

> *(***PAULY***,* **SHARKY***,* **LOU***, and* **BARBIE JO** *each take a side of the cake tray and lift. The boys sway precariously – first to one side, then to the other. The women manage to right the cake and get it moving back in the right direction. They step carefully into the kitchen.* **SHARKY** *and* **PAULY** *look over their shoulders nervously toward the front. Then catch each other's eye and grin.* **DARLENE** *continues primping.)*
>
> *(Lights dim, but just long enough to get the cake off the stage and the gangsters to remove their aprons and put their jackets back on. Then action continues.)*

Scene Three

LOU. (*Returns from loading the cake and removes her apron.*) It slid right in. No problems. First thing's gone right all day.

DARLENE. Really?

LOU. Smooth sailin' now, honey! Let's get you to the church.

> (*As she finishes speaking her line, the bell on the front door rings and* **LESTER** *returns. He wears a long church robe over his regular clothes.*)

LESTER. I gotta church full of people looking for Darlene and Jimmy. Are you coming or not?

DARLENE. Jimmy's not there?

LESTER. Not yet. I thought he'd be here.

DARLENE. Oh, Lou…

LOU. Now, don't panic. He'll show. I know it.

> (**BARBIE JO** *returns through the kitchen door.*)

BARBI JO. Lester, shouldn't you be at the church?

LESTER. I was just asking Lou and Darlene the same thing.

BARBIE JO. The cake's loaded, and we're on our way now.

DARLENE. Jimmy's not at the church, Barbie Jo! I've been jilted!

BARBIE JO. He's not?

LESTER. I'm sure he's on his way.

BARBIE JO. Why sure he is!

> (*Aside to* **LOU.**)

I hate to bring this up, but isn't there something you wanted to discuss with Lester in his other capacity?

LOU. (*Indicates* **DARLENE.**) Not now, Barbie Jo. Darlene's upset. It can wait.

BARBIE JO. Darlene's been upset all day, and I'm not sure this can wait.

LESTER. My other capacity?

LOU. Never mind, Lester. It'll wait.

BARBIE JO. Darlene, honey, why don't you come with me, and we'll get you and that dress all tucked in to the van snug as a bug in a rug.

>   *(DARLENE rises and smooths her skirt.)*

SHARKY. *(Returns from kitchen, followed by PAULY.)* You dames okay?

>   *(Sees LESTER.)*

Who's dis?

PAULY. You okay, Darlene?

DARLENE. *(Stands and falls into PAULY's arms.)* Jimmy's not at the church!

LESTER. Lester Thompson. Officiating at the wedding

SHARKY. Man of the cloth, eh?

PAULY. That explains the dress.

LESTER. It isn't a dress. It's a ministerial robe. I wear it to set the tone for the service.

PAULY. Like Father Giuseppi at St. Mark's, eh, boss?

SHARKY. We're pretty sure he wore dresses too, but they usually included pearls and heels. No matter.

LESTER. I hate to cut this short, but I have a church full of people waiting for a wedding. It'd be nice if we could get the bride and groom there sometime today!

LOU. Yeah, let's go. Everybody in the van. We'll take the short cut across Pullman's field. He won't...

>   *(Bell rings again, and the boys rush in. JIMMY is in the lead. All three are covered with mud and look a fright.)*

JIMMY. *(To DAVE and BILL.)* Told you she was here!

>   *(To DARLENE.)*

Darlene! Honey!

DARLENE. Don't you honey me, Jimmy Weaver. How dare you jilt me and then show up here late for our wedding looking like one of your hogs!

DAVE. Jilt! See, I told you. Funny word.

BARBIE JO. David Andrew Jackson Fox! Where have you been?

DAVE. *(Sarcastic.)* At a ladies' tea! Where do you think, Barbie Jo. We were fetchin' Jimmy.

BARBIE JO. And just where was Jimmy? A pigsty?

BILL. Just where we thought. He went to the cabin.

BARBIE JO. The Christmas cabin?

DAVE. That's the one.

LOU. That you under all that muck, Bill Wexler?

BILL. Yes'm, it is.

LOU. Is that your tuxedo?

BILL. Yes'm, it is.

LOU. You got anything to say for yourself?

BILL. No'm, I don't.

DAVE. Well I do! I know this looks bad, but you can't be mad at us!

LOU. And why not?

DAVE. Cuz, look! We got him!

BARBIE JO. *(Sarcastic.)* Looks like he came along peaceable like. What'd ya have to do? Mud wrestle him?

DAVE. No, we didn't have no trouble with Jimmy.

BARBIE JO. Then how'd you get so filthy?

DARLENE. *(To* **DAVE**.*)* You didn't?

DAVE. Nope. Once we talked some sense to him, he wanted to come back. He was even sorry he left, but...

LOU. Why is there always a "but"?

BILL. But, the early thaw made them mountain roads awful muddy. Jimmy's truck sank in and blocked our way.

DAVE. Fortunately, my dual quad hemi eight valve handles muddy terrain and just about everything else known to man.

BARBIE JO. For what you paid for that monstrosity, it should walk on water!

DAVE. Now, honey, if it weren't for that fabulous truck, we'd still be stuck on the mountain.

BARBIE JO. I know I'm gonna regret askin', but just how did super truck save the day?

DAVE. At first, we were sure we'd be stuck there for good, but then Bill...

LOU. *(To* **SHARKY** *and* **PAULY***.)* That'd be the tall mud man over there. My husband, Bill. Bill, this is Sharky and Pauly.

BILL. *(Extends his hand and sees all the mud. Pulls it back and wipes it on his pants.)* Sorry 'bout that. Nice to meet ya! You boys in for the weddin'?

SHARKY. We were just headin' to the church.

DAVE. Pleased to meet ya. Anyhow... Bill remembered them big loggin' chains in the old mining shack. We chained the trucks together, and I used mine to pull Jimmy's little farm toy outta the mud.

JIMMY. Hey! What'd I tell you about pickin' on my truck?

BILL. He's right. You promised to be nice if we made it home in one piece, and here we are.

JIMMY. Besides, we needed both trucks to get outta that mud.

BARBIE JO. You mean you got these yahoos to work together?

BILL. T'weren't easy.

LOU. That's obvious.

DAVE. Sorry about the mud, Lou. We'll mop up after the wedding.

DARLENE. Well who says there's gonna be a wedding?

ALL BUT DARLENE. What? Huh? No wedding?

DARLENE. I didn't particularly enjoy being jilted today, Jimmy Weaver!

JIMMY. And I didn't particularly enjoy doing it, Darlene. Geesh, honey, I made a mistake. I focused on all the wrong things, and that was...er, wrong. Now, I'm focused on all the right things, and I'm sorry.

DARLENE. You are?

JIMMY. I am. I'm sorry I hurt you, and I'm sorry I made the wrong choice and ran off this morning.

DARLENE. *(Cute pouty lip.)* Choice?

JIMMY. Bill helped me see that. He said the choice is up to me. I can choose to worry and get myself all worked up, or I can choose to be happy. Either way, the choice is mine. Darlene, if you can forgive me, I choose you.

DARLENE. Oh, Jimmy

> *(To* **LOU**.*)*

You were right, Lou.

LOU. I usually am. About what?

DARLENE. Having faith.

LOU. Oh, that.

DARLENE. You knew Jimmy'd be back. You kept tellin' me, and I almost didn't believe it. I didn't have faith.

JIMMY. *(Puts an arm around* **LOU**.*)* You told her I'd come back?

LOU. I did. When it comes to lovin' Darlene, ain't no one more dependable than you, Jimmy Weaver.

JIMMY. But why?

LOU. I know your heart. I know you've loved Darlene since the first time you set eyes on her. You two belong together. Two sides of the same coin. Right, Lester?

LESTER. Yes, ma'am.

JIMMY. We do belong together.

> *(To* **DARLENE** *as he falls to one knee.)*

Darlene, please, forgive me. Marry me. I've been an awful fool and ruined your whole day, but I have my whole life to make it up to you. Give me another chance.

DARLENE. Oh, Jimmy! Are you sure? Are you really sure, because I could never be happy if I thought you weren't happy.

JIMMY. Honey, I'm gonna be happy every day of my life now that we'll be together.

DARLENE. That's just about the sweetest thing I ever heard!

JIMMY. It's a choice, Darlene. I choose to spend the rest of my life with you!

LESTER. Now that that's settled, maybe we could move this soiree over to the church where your guests are waitin'.

BILL. What about our clothes?

DAVE. We should probably hose off first.

JIMMY. I wouldn't mind a quick shower myself.

PAULY. *(On impulse pulls his hand gun and points it at* **JIMMY.***)* You ain't goin' nowhere, pal.

DARLENE. Pauly!

BARBIE JO. *(Sarcastic to* **LOU.***)* You thought our news for Lester could wait, huh?

SHARKY. What you's up to, Pauly?

PAULY. Darlene's our friend. He ran off once. What's to keep him from doin' it again? I say we take her with us to the hideout and keep him from breakin' her heart again.

LESTER. Take Darlene! What's this all about?

LOU. Don't you boys need to lay low – go unnoticed?

PAULY. Yeah.

LOU. You really think you're gonna go unnoticed trailin' this in your wake?

(Gestures to **DARLENE** *as she fluffs her dress.)*

SHARKY. She's got a point, Pauly. As much as I like her, I don't think we should take the bride. Might be bad luck.

PAULY. But, boss, he ran off on her.

SHARKY. And now he's back. Why'd you come back, Jimmy?

PAULY. Yeah, why'd you come back, Jimmy?

JIMMY. Because I realized I'd made a big mistake. Didn't you ever make a mistake and want to fix it?

SHARKY. Sure, kid. Sure I did.

JIMMY. Please, don't keep me from fixin' this one. Please, don't take my Darlene!

PAULY. I don't know. I don't trust him, boss. He's got shifty eyes. Let's take Darlene and keep her safe.

DARLENE. Pauly, I know you want to help, but taking me away from my friends and my Jimmy... That's not the answer. You don't want to do this.

PAULY. Are you sure?

DARLENE. 'Course I am! I forgive Jimmy. I'm ready to start singin' "Get Me to the Church On Time"!

BILL, LOU, BARBIE JO & DAVE. No! Not that! You don't have to sing, Darlene!

PAULY. I've got a better idea.

BARBIE JO. Uh-oh.

PAULY. We got the minister. We got the bride and the groom. I say we make him go through with it now so there's no more cold feet.

LESTER. Something tells me these fellas're what you wanted to tell me about, Lou.

LOU. Lester, these are Darlene's new friends. They just arrived today. They may need to make your professional acquaintance, and they ain't Methodists.

LESTER. I see that.

DARLENE. They're good boys. Really they are. Sharky here baked the new tiers for my cake after Dave's dog ate 'em.

LESTER. These are the boys from the kitchen earlier?

BARBIE JO. We didn't know about their other interests then.

LESTER. Seems I heard you boys are wanted for questioning by federal officials.

SHARKY. (*Pulls his own gun and covers* **LESTER**.) How'd you hear a thing like that?

LESTER. It's a small town. News travels.

SHARKY. I see that. Just when we was startin' to feel welcome. Nice people. Good hooch. Too bad word's out. How 'bout we just excuse ourselves and forget we ever met?

PAULY. No, boss. He's gonna marry Darlene if it's the last thing he does.

DARLENE. No, Pauly. Not like this.

SHARKY. The kid's gotta point. Our wedding gift to you. We make sure he marries you now. Then we'll be on our way. You's can always get married again in a classy joint later.

PAULY. One of those nice drive-through chapels in Vegas or Atlantic City. I always wanted to have Elvis sing at my wedding.

DARLENE. Me too! But, really, this isn't necessary.

PAULY. I say it is! Minister, make with the words.

LOU. Sharky, think about this.

SHARKY. It's not up to me now, Miss Lou. Once the kid sets his mind to something, he's like a dog with a bone. It can't hurt. Have a ceremony here, now for your friends and do it again at the church for everybody else.

BARBIE JO. He's got a point there. Your real friends are all right here.

DARLENE. But my cousins...

DAVE. Are probably half in the bag already.

PAULY. *(To **LESTER**.)* Come on... Dearly beloved.

LESTER. Excuse me.

PAULY. I ain't stupid, mister. Weddings always start, "Dearly beloved..."

LESTER. *(To **JIMMY** and **DARLENE**.)* Is this okay with you?

JIMMY. It's better than the alternative.

LESTER. *(Accepting.)* Okay then. Dearly beloved...

DARLENE. Wait. Lou, you're here. Next to me. Barbie Jo there.

> *(She grabs **BILL**'s arm.)*

Bill, you come around this way. Oh, that's still wet, isn't it?

BILL. Sorry, Darlene. Don't get it on your dress.

DARLENE. And Dave, you're there.

> *(She points.)*

Okay, Lester. Now we're ready.

LESTER. Dearly beloved, we are gathered here today to unite this man and this woman in holy matrimony. If any man present can give just cause why these two should not be united in marriage, let him speak now or forever hold his peace.

> *(The room is silent as **PAULY** swings his gun at each to make sure no one speaks. After an uncomfortable pause…)*

Well, good.

Now, Darlene, do you take Jimmy to be your lawful wedded husband? To have and to hold from this day forward, forsaking all others, and keeping only unto him 'til death do you part?

DARLENE. *(Joyous.)* I do!

LESTER. And do you, Jimmy, take Darlene to be your lawful wedded wife? To have and to hold from this day forward, forsaking all others, and keeping only unto her 'til death do you part?

JIMMY. I sure do!

DAVE. *(Aside to **BILL**.)* I always knew Jimmy'd end up gettin' married at the wrong end of a shotgun!

BARBIE JO. Hush, Dave! Pay attention!

LESTER. Then…

> *(He unzips his robe and shows his Sheriff's badge underneath.)*

As county sheriff, I hereby declare you men under arrest! Grab 'em, Bill!

> *(He drops his Bible, pulls his gun, and **BILL** and **DAVE** move to subdue **SHARKY** and **PAULY**. There's a brief struggle, which **BILL** and **DAVE** win, taking their guns and holding them by the arms. **LESTER** produces two pairs of handcuffs, which he passes to **BILL** and **DAVE**. They cuff **SHARKY** and **PAULY**.)*

SHARKY. You's can't do that! We're wedding guests!

PAULY. Darlene!

LOU. How'd you know?

LESTER. I didn't. But any time an APB comes through, I keep my badge and gun close, just in case. Someone call Dalton!

BARBIE JO. I've got it. So, wait, are they married or not?

> *(Takes out her cell phone and mimes a call to Dalton as she waits for his answer.)*

LESTER. Not yet, but we'll take care of that after Dalton picks up the prisoners. We'll consider this a rehearsal.

SHARKY. What's gonna happen to us?

LESTER. You'll be turned over for questioning. If there's no grounds to hold you, you'll be released.

SHARKY. *(Sheepishly.)* And if there are?

LESTER. You're my prisoners. I'll make sure you get the best treatment possible and a good local lawyer.

PAULY. You'd do that for us?

LESTER. Why sure. You helped Darlene when she needed it. Happy to return the favor.

SHARKY. But you's a cop.

PAULY. And we pulled a gun on you.

LOU. Sharky, remember earlier when we were telling Darlene she needed to have faith in people.

SHARKY. Yeah.

LOU. You can have faith in Lester. If he says he'll help you, he means it.

PAULY. I never had faith in no cop before.

DARLENE. *(Gently.)* Maybe it's time to start.

BARBIE JO. I hear they have a terrific food services department at the state pen.

> *(To **SHARKY**.)*

You could teach those boys a thing or two about baking cakes.

PAULY. You girls could bring some of Uncle Jedediah's secret ingredient on visiting days.

BARBIE JO. Only if we wanted to join you behind bars.

BILL. Uncle Jedediah? How'd he get involved in cake baking?

DAVE. Ain't he the moonshiner?

LOU. It's a long story, boys. Let's just say Darlene's cousins are probably enjoying this wedding day way more than anybody else.

SHARKY. This might be just the vacation I've been needing.

> *(Sees movement out the window.)*

That looks like our ride.

BILL. Let's go.

DAVE. Come on.

> *(Takes **SHARKY** out the door and hands him over to someone who is supposed to be **LESTER**'s deputy. He does not need to be seen.)*

PAULY. Darlene, I hope you two will be very happy.

DARLENE. *(Kisses him gently on the cheek.)* Thank you, Pauly. We're gonna be just fine.

> *(**BILL** takes **PAULY** out to the deputy as well. **LESTER** follows.)*

LOU. Well, if this ain't been quite the day!

BARBIE JO. Darlene, next time you get married, do us all a favor and go to Vegas!

DARLENE. What? And miss all this?

> *(**BILL** and **DAVE** return, followed by **LESTER**.)*

LESTER. Can we go to the church now before Darlene's cousins tear the place apart?

JIMMY. Sounds great to me!

DARLENE. No.

JIMMY. No? Why not? You ain't still mad, are ya, honey?

DARLENE. No. I ain't mad. I've just been thinkin'.

BARBIE JO. There's a first.

DARLENE. All my best memories… All my happiest times… Pretty much all the things and people that make me happiest are right here in this room.

LOU. *(Her turn to cry.)* Oh, Darlene!

DARLENE. And after today, I won't be a waitress here no more. I'll be Mrs. Jimmy Weaver – hog farmer! Lester, do you think it would be awful selfish if we finish the ceremony here and go over to the church for the reception?

LESTER. I think it would be absolutely wonderful, Darlene!

DARLENE. *(To JIMMY.)* Do you mind?

JIMMY. Havin' our wedding in Lou's Diner? Can't think of anywhere else I'd rather be!

DAVE. 'Cept maybe Earl's Pub & Grub at Happy Hour.

BARBIE JO. Hush, Dave.

LESTER. Okay, everybody get in place.

> *(DAVE starts to move to the wrong spot.)*

BARBIE JO. *(Points.)* No, Dave, you're there.

> *(They move to their appropriate spots.)*

LESTER. Ready?
Now where were we? Oh yes…
Jimmy, do you have the ring?

JIMMY. *(To BILL.)* I forgot! The ring!

BILL. Calm down. It's right here.

> *(He produces a small box from his tux pocket and hands the ring to JIMMY.)*

JIMMY. Thought we lost it in the mud.

DAVE. So did I.

LESTER. Repeat after me. With this ring, I thee wed.

JIMMY. With this ring, I thee wed.

LESTER. And pledge too my troth.

JIMMY. And pledge too my troth.

DAVE. *(Whispers loudly.)* Does anybody know what that means?

BARBIE JO. Shhh!

DAVE. I'm just sayin', he's pledgin' something, and he don't even know what it is. Don't seem smart.

BARBIE JO. Shhhhhh!!

LESTER. Darlene, do you have your ring?

DARLENE. Lou?

LOU. Right here, honey!

(Hands the ring to **DARLENE.***)*

LESTER. Darlene, repeat after me. With this ring, I thee wed.

DARLENE. With this ring, I thee wed.

LESTER. And pledge too my troth.

DARLENE. And pledge too my troth.

BARBIE JO. See. She pledges hers too, so it all works out.

LESTER. In as much as Jimmy and Darlene have pledged their hearts and exchanged these rings to signify their deep and abiding love, I now declare them husband and wife. Let what God has joined together not be torn asunder.

BARBIE JO. *(To* **DAVE.***)* You remember what that means, don't ya?

LESTER. *(Pause.)* Whatcha waitin' on, Jim? You may now kiss the bride!

JIMMY. Well, I'll be! Ya don't have to tell me twice!

(Kisses **DARLENE.***)*

We're hitched.

(Pulls **DARLENE** *into a full-body embrace. When she comes out of it, it would be terrific if she can be coated in the mud that was on the front of* **JIMMY.***)*

BARBIE JO. Ain't it beautiful?

LOU. Except the mud, yes.

(Pause.)

Barbie Jo, we don't have anything more exciting than water to toast the happy couple, but I feel we should do something.

BARBIE JO. I'll grab the pitcher.

(The water pitcher must be ceramic or some other substance that the audience cannot see through.)

LOU. I'll get some glasses.

DAVE. Never thought I'd see the day. Jimmy Weaver married.

JIMMY. Never been happier, Dave. It's true what they say – I feel like I finally found my better half.

BILL. In this instance, it's probably true.

(BARBIE JO returns with the water pitcher filled with grape juice, and LOU carries a tray of clear water glasses. The pitcher should not be clear so the audience believes it holds just water.)

LOU. Here, Bill, hold this. Help me pour the water out so we can toast Darlene and Jimmy.

(She begins to pour and is shocked when the liquid comes out looking like wine.)

Barbie Jo, I thought you said this pitcher was full of water.

BARBIE JO. It was, Lou. I swear. I filled it myself this morning before we started on the cakes.

LESTER. *(Sips.)* Water into wine at a wedding!

DAVE. *(Sips.)* Nice vintage too!

LESTER. Haven't heard that one in a while.

LOU. Just another not-so-ordinary day here at Lou's Diner.

BARBIE JO. I don't understand. How'd it turn to wine?

BILL. Some things in life aren't supposed to be understood, Barbie Jo. Ain't that right, Lester.

LESTER. Never look a gift horse in the mouth, Bill.

(Drinks again and smiles.)

DARLENE. Getting Jimmy to the altar's miracle enough for me.

JIMMY. Cheers!

> *(They all drink from their water glasses and toast the happy couple.)*

ALL. Cheers!

> *(DAVE moves to BARBIE JO's side, and LOU moves to BILL's side. The men put an arm around their wives.)*

BILL. Reminds me of us when we were that age.

LOU. We were never that age, but thanks just the same.

JIMMY. Come on, y'all! We're goin' to a party!

DARLENE. I'm now officially Mrs. Jimmy Weaver!

JIMMY. And I'm now officially Mr. Jimmy Weaver…er, Darlene's husband!

BARBIE JO. The place won't be the same without you, Darlene.

DARLENE. Don't worry, Barbie Jo. Jimmy says I can come back any time you need me.

DAVE. *(Aside.)* Mostly around butchering time.

BILL. Did Darlene's cousins show up for the wedding?

LOU. Sure. Why?

DAVE. It's been a heck of a day already. Knowing the Fulmer clan, I'd bet the party's just gettin' started.

BARBIE JO. Well, with Uncle Jed's special recipe in the cake, there won't be no complainin' about the food!

BILL. Dave's right. With Darlene's cousins in town, this is just the start of a good old fashioned redneck country wedding!

> *(Raises his glass again.)*

Here's to the bride and groom!

> *(Drinks.)*

Pretty good wine for water.

DAVE, LESTER, LOU & BARBIE JO. The bride and groom!

(**JIMMY** *and* **DARLENE** *kiss and lights fade.*)

BARBIE JO. *(To* **DAVE.***)* I love me a happy ending, don't you?
(Curtain.)

www.ingramcontent.com/pod-product-compliance
Lightning Source LLC
Chambersburg PA
CBHW070359120726
47909CB00008B/2914